THE GREAT HAMSTER MASSACRE

Katie Davies

Illustrated by Hannah Shaw

SIMON AND SCHUSTER

A big thank you to my Mum and Dad, and my husband, Alan, and my agent, Clare Conville, for all their help.

First published in Great Britain in 2010 by Simon and Schuster UK Ltd,
a CBS company.

Text copyright © 2010 Katie Davies
Cover and interior illustrations copyright © 2010 Hannah Shaw

Simon & Schuster UK Ltd
1st Floor, 222 Gray's Inn Road, London WC1X 8HB

A CIP catalogue record for this book is available from the British Library.

978-1-84738-595-6

5 7 9 10 8 6 4

Printed and bound in Great Britain.

www.simonandschuster.co.uk
www.katiedaviesbooks.com

For Daniel

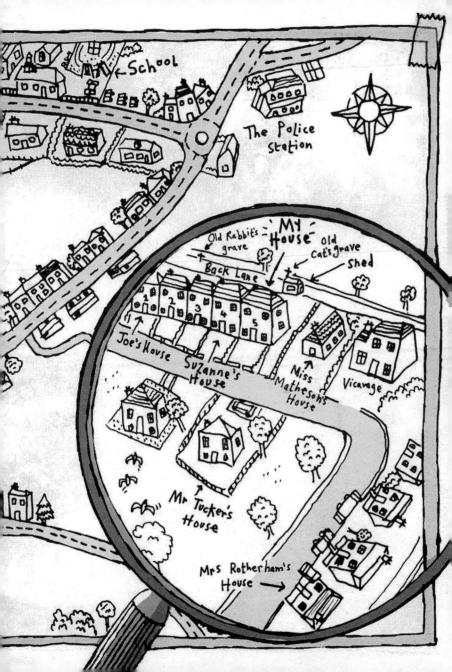

CHAPTER 1
What A Massacre Is

This is a story about me, and Tom, and our Investigation into the Hamster Massacre. I'm supposed to be writing my What-I-Did-In-The-Summer-Holidays Story for school, but I'm going to write this story first because you should always write a Real Investigation up straight away. That's what my friend Suzanne says. And Suzanne knows everything about Real Investigations. Mum said she didn't think my teacher would like the story of my real summer holidays, and how the Hamster Massacre happened.

She said, 'Anna (that's my name), *some* nice things must have happened this holidays and if you can't remember any, you can make some nice things up, and put them in your summer holiday report instead.'

Mum doesn't think it matters if my holiday report isn't exactly true, but Graham Roberts got in trouble last time when he put that he spent the whole holiday in the dog-basket. His dog had died, so maybe he *did* stay in the dog-basket all holiday, but Mrs Peters said he must have come out to eat and go to the toilet and things like that, and Joe-down-the-road told Tom he saw Graham at Cubs. And you can't be in a dog basket *there*.

Tom is my little brother. I've got another brother too, and a sister, but they're older than me and Tom and they don't really care about hamsters much, so they're not in this story. Tom is four years younger than me, except for a little while every year after he has his birthday, and before I have mine, when he is only *three* years younger. But most of the time he's four years younger, so it's best to say that.

Anyway, me and Tom are not supposed to talk about the hamsters and what happened to them anymore because it's best to try to forget about it all, and stop exaggerating, and making it worse than it actually was, and all that. But we couldn't do that anyway because massacres can't really get any worse than they are. That is the point of them.

This is what it says about massacres in my dictionary...

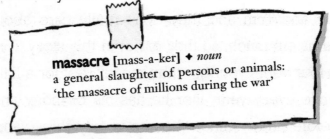

massacre [mass-a-ker] ✦ *noun*
a general slaughter of persons or animals:
'the massacre of millions during the war'

The dictionary in Suzanne's house said you could have another kind of massacre. It said...

massacre [mass-a-ker] ✦ *informal*
a bad defeat, especially in sport: 'England was massacred 5-0 by France in the semi-final'

But the Hamster Massacre was not that kind of massacre. The Hamster Massacre was definitely a *formal* kind of massacre.

10

I will keep the story of the Hamster Massacre in the shed with the worms, and the wasp trap, and the pictures that we traced from Joe-down-the-road's Mum's book. Me and Suzanne have made a lock for the shed door, and we've got a new password. We are the only ones allowed in the shed, except when we let Tom in, but he gets bored when we are making the locks and deciding on the passwords and stuff, and he is too little for the pictures from Joe's Mum's book so, most of the time, when we go in the shed, Tom goes in the house and has a biscuit.

❧ CHAPTER 2 ❧
The Wall And The Window

Suzanne lives next door. Her surname is Barry. The wall between our house and the Barrys' house is thin. We can hear the Barrys through the wall. We hear them when they scrape their plates, and when they flush the loo, and we hear their Dad shout,

'YOU BETTER GET DOWN THESE STAIRS BEFORE I HAVE TO COME UP!'

Mum says, imagine what the Barrys can hear from our house. But none of the Barrys heard anything unusual the day the massacre happened.

Last summer holidays, me and Suzanne made a plan for getting through the wall. Our bedrooms are right next to each other so, if I made a hole on my side of the wall, under my bed, and Suzanne made a hole in exactly the same place on her side of the wall, under her bed, the two holes would meet in the middle to make a tunnel. We wrote the plan on the back of a roll of wallpaper in the shed. Suzanne made a list of all the tools we needed, and I drew the diagrams with arrows on.

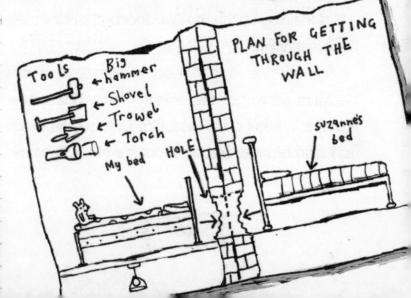

PLAN FOR GETTING THROUGH THE WALL

Tools
Big ← hammer
← Shovel
← Trowel
← Torch
My bed
HOLE
suzanne's bed

When we had finished, Suzanne wanted to do the diagrams again because she is a better drawer than I am, and then we fell out, so I took all the tools and hid them, and then Suzanne took the plan and hid that.

And Suzanne's Dad found the plan, and he looked under Suzanne's bed, and he saw that the paint had been picked off the wall, and that a hole had been made in the plaster, and now me and Suzanne aren't allowed to play in Suzanne's room **'EVER AGAIN!'**

I don't ring on the Barrys' doorbell if Suzanne's Dad is at home.

Anyway, we don't need a tunnel anymore because we've got a Knocking Code. This is how it works. When I go to bed, I knock three times on my bedroom wall and, if the coast is clear, Suzanne knocks back three times, and then we both go to our windows and we open them and crawl out and sit outside on the ledge in the night.

Suzanne knows the names of all the stars like The Plough and Orion's Belt, and how to spot them, but she always points to a different place, and I never see anything that looks like a plough. I just say that I can.

Orions
Starry
BELT →

The Plough?
← Ursa Major

Sometimes we see Mr Tucker opposite standing by his window too. Mr Tucker's got a lot of medals from The War. He is easier to spot than The Plough. Normally, when Mr Tucker's at his window, he's looking out for people doing things he doesn't like, like burgling, or fighting, or dropping litter. Then he comes out of his house and tells them to stop. Especially if it's litter.

Anyway, me and Suzanne have to be careful when we climb out on the window ledge now, especially if we spot Mr Tucker, because he could tell Suzanne's Dad, and Suzanne's Dad says if he finds out she's been out there again she will have to swap bedrooms with her brother. He's called Carl but he isn't in this story because he's only a baby.

CHAPTER 3
The New Cat

Before me and Tom got the hamsters, there were a lot of reasons why we weren't allowed to have any. The first reason was the cat. Our cat is not an ordinary cat that sits by the fire and lets you stroke her, and that is because she is from a farm where she was a Wild Cat. We used to have another cat and it was a much better one. But it got run over by Miss Matheson in the back lane. Miss Matheson doesn't like it if you go in her bit of the back lane. She says, **'PRIVATE PROPERTY! PRIVATE PROPERTY!'** And bangs on the window.

Miss Matheson never admitted that she ran

over the Old Cat but me and Tom know it was her because it was outside her house. And anyway, Suzanne saw cat blood on Miss Matheson's car tyres.

Before she got run over, the Old Cat used to let you do anything. You could wrap her in a blanket, put a hat on her, put her in a pram, and walk her down the road and she didn't even miaow.

You couldn't put the New Cat in a pram. You can't put the New Cat in anything, not even in its own basket, unless you've got gardening gloves on.

I bet Miss Matheson wishes she never killed the Old Cat because when it isn't hunting, or asleep with one eye open, the New Cat spends its time walking slowly up and down in front of Miss Matheson's gate. And it drives her dog mad.

Miss Matheson asked Mum if we could keep the cat inside but you can't keep the New Cat anywhere.

The New Cat hunts. Its bowl is always full of cat food, *special* cat food from small silver tins that the Old Cat only used to get at Christmas, but it still hunts. It hunts birds, mice, and Joe-down-the-road's New Rabbit.

It tried to hunt Joe's Old Rabbit too but as soon as it saw our New Cat, Joe's Old Rabbit panicked, and died.

Joe's Mum's Boyfriend looked at Joe's Old Rabbit and said, **'Heart attack. I'll get a trowel.'**

And he did, and he dug a hole in the back lane, and he put the Old Rabbit in the hole.

Joe didn't like seeing the soil go on the Old Rabbit's fur because when it was alive the Old Rabbit was very fussy about its fur, and it hated getting anything on it, and when it *did* get anything on it, like soil, or bits of carrot, it cleaned it off straight away.

I thought the Old Rabbit would rather have been put in a shoebox on some straw, with a dandelion, before it got put in the hole, but Joe's Mum's Boyfriend told me to be quiet.

Joe cried a lot because of the soil, and the fur, and because he wasn't allowed to even wipe it away from the Old Rabbit's eyes or mouth. And he knew the Old Rabbit would hate it.

Me and Suzanne told Joe that as soon as his Mum's Boyfriend went home, and stopped staying at his house, we would dig the Old Rabbit up, and clean its fur, and put it in a box, and make a cross to go in the ground behind it, like the Old Cat has.

But Joe kept on crying,

'GET THE SOIL OUT HIS EYES...
GET THE SOIL OUT HIS EYES...'

and his Mum's Boyfriend sent us home.

●ξ ●ξ ●ξ

Anyway, when there aren't any birds or mice outside, and Joe is guarding his New Rabbit with a Super Soaker, and Miss Matheson won't let her dog in the garden, and the New Cat is sick of hunting spiders, and stones, and the wind, it sometimes wants to come in the house.

The New Cat doesn't stop hunting once it's inside the house and has finished fighting with the cat flap, either. Its best things for hunting inside the house are feet. It likes bare feet best, then in socks, then in slippers. If all the feet in the house are in shoes, and it is raining outside, it will also hunt the hoover, the spider plants and the sound of the Barrys' loo flushing.

Mum said that wherever we might put a hamster, in whatever kind of a cage, with however many guards, if the New Cat couldn't scare it to death she would hunt it and kill it in some other way.

She said, 'You and your brother may as well kill a hamster yourselves as bring one within a mile of the New Cat.'

I can't remember every single other reason why we weren't allowed the hamsters before we got them, but I know that the New Cat was Reason Number One.

⁂ CHAPTER 4 ⁂
Reasons And Real Reasons

A lot of times, when someone tells you a reason why you can't have something, the reason isn't really true. Like when Mum tells Tom he can't have a Two Ball Screwball from the Ice Cream Man because the Ice Cream Man hasn't got any left. That reason isn't true. The *real* reason is that Two Ball Screwballs have got bubblegum in, and Tom is too young for bubblegum. Last time he had some he squished it in the bath mat.

Out of all the reasons for why somebody can't have something, being too young is the worst, so when 'too young' is the real reason, Mum mostly makes another one up instead.

Other times, when someone tells you a reason why you can't have something, the reason might be true, but it still might not be the real reason why they don't want you to have it. Like when Suzanne's Dad told Suzanne that she couldn't have any pets because he was allergic to pet hair. That's true, Suzanne's Dad *is* allergic to pet hair. It makes his nose run and his eyes itch and his face go red. And that's why the Barrys had to send their dog Barney to live on a farm. But it isn't the *real* reason why he won't let Suzanne have any pets. The real reason is because he *hates* pets. It was Tom who found that out.

In our house, Tom gets told more reasons for why he can't have things than anyone else. So all Tom does, whenever he gets told a reason, is think of something else he wants as fast as he can instead. So, when me and Suzanne told Tom all about how Suzanne wasn't allowed any pets because her Dad was allergic to pet hair, Tom said, 'What about a tortoise? They don't have hairs on.'

Suzanne thought about all the pets she'd asked for. A dog, a cat, a rabbit, a guinea pig, a hamster and a budgie (a budgie doesn't have hair exactly but her Dad said he is allergic to feathers too) and she hadn't ever even *asked* for a pet without hair like a tortoise.

So we thought of some pets that don't have hair on and we started to make a list.

ANNA'S AND TOM'S AND SUZANNE'S LIST OF PETS WITH NO HAIRS ON THAT SUZANNE'S DAD WON'T BE ALLERGIC TO

1. Tortoise
2. Frog
3. Snake
4. Stick Insect
5. Eel
6. Fish
7. Terrapin (a small tortoise that likes water)
8. Lizard

We couldn't think of any more pets with no hair on, so we went on the computer and we put 'pets with no hairs' in, and guess what? You can get dogs and cats and rabbits and guinea pigs and rats and hamsters and every single kind of pet there is without any hair on if you want it. There was a cat with no hairs on called a Sphinx, like the statues in Egypt that we did at school with Mrs Peters, and there were five kinds of dogs with no hairs on called Hairless Dogs, each with their own special name. Some of them are too hard to say, and they probably aren't even in English, but I'll write them down anyway.

HAIRLESS DOGS

1. Peruvian Inca Orchid
2. Hairless Chinese Crested
3. Hairless Khalla
4. American Hairless Terrier
5. Xoloitzcuintli

When Suzanne's Mum came to make her go home, we showed her the Hairless Dogs List and the pictures on the computer. When she saw the first ones she screamed and said 'Ugh! They look like aliens!' But when she saw the one called American Hairless Terrier, she said, 'Oh', and she looked sad and put her head on one side and said, 'That's the same kind of dog as Barney.'

It didn't look like Barney to me. But Suzanne's Mum said it was 'exactly like Barney. But bald.' My Mum said a bald dog was better than no dog, and Suzanne's Mum said, 'Same with men' and Suzanne's Mum and My Mum laughed a lot then, for ages, even though it isn't that funny. My Dad is bald. So is Suzanne's.

Suzanne's Mum said to Suzanne that if it was okay with her Dad, they could get a bald dog.

29

It wasn't okay with Suzanne's Dad, though, because we heard him shouting through the wall. He shouted louder than ever,

'I DON'T CARE ABOUT THE HAIR...'

He said,

'I JUST HATE PETS!'

And everyone went quiet because you can't ask, 'What about a tortoise?' after a reason like that.

🐾 CHAPTER 5 🐾
Hamster Horror

Although the New Cat was always Reason Number One for us not being allowed a hamster, it turned out not to be the real reason after all.

One night, after tea, when me and Tom didn't eat our onions and we had go to our rooms until we were ready to say sorry to Mum for making sick noises, we got thinking about hamsters, and how it was all the New Cat's fault that we weren't allowed to have one. So we made a plan, and we went downstairs where Mum was watching telly with Nanna.

And I said, 'We are sorry about the onions, Mum.'

Mum didn't say anything because 'Coronation Street' was on and, even though she says she doesn't even like 'Coronation Street', and only puts it on for Nanna, she never likes talking when it's on.

Anyway, Tom said, 'Could we have a hamster if the New Cat was dead, or didn't live at our house for a different reason?'

Mum said, 'Mmm… what?' and then she said, 'No!'

And Tom said, 'Why?', which is Tom's favourite question.

And Mum said, 'Because. New Cat or no New Cat, hamsters are bad news.'

And Tom said, 'Why?' again.

And Mum said, 'Because.'

And then she said, 'Bed.'

And Tom said, 'Why?'

And Mum said, 'Right!' And she stopped watching 'Coronation Street' and she stood up and said, 'Ten... Nine... Eight...'

And, then Nanna said, 'Quick, go on up, Duck, and I'll come up too, and I'll tell you a story.'

And Tom said 'Is it about hamsters?'

And Nanna said, 'Yes, it is. It's all about what happened to two little hamsters your Mum knew, and why they were both bad news.'

Mum had never told us anything about knowing any hamsters, so we ran up and got ready as quickly as we could, and Tom let me brush his teeth, because he takes ages when he does it himself, and he doesn't even brush really, he just eats the toothpaste, and we got in Tom's bed and we waited for Nanna. Which took quite a long time because of Nanna's hips, and the stairs, and because Mum had to help her.

☙ CHAPTER 6 ☙
Geoff And The Sliding Double Doors

The first hamster Nanna told us all about was called Geoff. Geoff was Mum's best friend Shirley's hamster, from when her and Shirley lived in the same street when they were girls. Shirley had six brothers in her house, and a hamster, and an extension, which was an extra bit on the back of the house that Mum's house didn't have. The extension had double sliding doors.

One day, Mum and Shirley and some of Shirley's brothers were playing with Geoff in the extension. Geoff was out of his cage, which Shirley's Mum didn't mind as long as Shirley and Mum picked his poos up after, and put them in the bin before Shirley's tea was ready.

But Shirley's youngest brother kept picking up Geoff's poos too, and chasing Mum and Shirley with them, and Mum and Shirley were screaming, and running in and out of the double sliding extension doors to escape from him, and Shirley's youngest brother was chasing them, and Mum and Shirley were screaming even more, and sliding the doors shut on Shirley's youngest brother as quickly as they could. And Geoff was running around too, because that's what hamsters do when they're allowed out of their cages.

And Mum ran towards the sliding doors and screamed and slid them open, and Shirley's brother ran after her. And Mum ran through the sliding doors into the garden, and screamed, and slid them shut.

And when she slid them shut she heard another little scream, from low down, and she looked to see what it was, and there, on *her* side of the door, in the garden, was the *front* half of Geoff. And she looked through the sliding doors, and there, on the *other* side of the door, in the extension, was the *back* half of Geoff. And the sliding doors were shut tight in-between.

CHAPTER 7
Bernard And The Cashmere Coat

The second hamster Nanna told us all about was called Bernard. Bernard was a big fat orange hamster with tiny black eyes that Dad bought Mum for her 21st birthday. Mum didn't really want a hamster for her 21st birthday but Dad bought her one because Shirley had told him all about how Mum had cut Geoff in half with the sliding doors when they were little girls, and how sad she had been, and Dad thought that maybe now she was grown up it would be funny if he bought her a hamster of her own.

Anyway, what Mum *really* wanted for her birthday was a green cashmere coat. She had seen the coat in the shops when she was in town with Shirley. It was the most beautiful, and the most green, and the most expensive coat that Mum and Shirley had ever seen, and Mum showed it to Dad every time they went past it.

← GREEN
+
EXPENSIVE

The night before Mum's birthday Dad told Mum that he had bought her a birthday present that was 'lovely and soft and warm', and Mum was sure it was the cashmere coat.

In the morning, when Dad gave Mum a big fat orange hamster, Mum was not very pleased. But she thought that, seeing as Dad had given her a hamster, she had better call it something. So she called it Bernard. And she put its cage on

the table in the kitchen, and she started doing lots of tidying and cleaning because she was having a birthday party that night.

When everything was nearly ready Mum took Bernard's cage off the table because Bernard looked like the least clean and tidy thing in the house, and she put Bernard's cage on the shelf under the coat hooks in the cupboard under the stairs. She looked at Bernard and thought, 'He's very nice really', and she remembered how much she liked Geoff, before she killed him by mistake, and she thought how nice it would be to have a hamster after all. She took Bernard out of his cage and she stroked him on his back, and he *was* very lovely, and very soft and very warm, and she kissed him on the head, and she put him back in the cage and she shut the cupboard door. And then the doorbell rang, and Mum went to answer it, and it was Shirley. She was wearing the green cashmere coat! She had walked past the shop that morning, and bought it half price in the sale.

½ PRICE

Shirley looked very nice in the coat. And Mum thought how nice *she* would have looked in it if it was *her* coat. Dad and Shirley laughed when Mum told them how she had thought Dad was getting her the coat for her birthday, and then he had given her a hamster. And Mum laughed too, but only a bit, because she didn't think it was all that funny. And she took Shirley's beautiful green cashmere coat, and she hung it up in the cupboard on the hooks above Bernard's cage.

When the party was over and it was time for everyone to go home, Mum went into the cupboard to get everyone's coats. She took down Shirley's green cashmere coat and was just thinking how beautiful, and how green, and how soft it was, when she noticed that in the back of the coat, just where Shirley's bum would be if she was wearing it, there was a hole.

She didn't remember the hole being there when she hung the coat up, and she was just wondering how it might have got there since, when she saw something in Bernard's cage. Right there, in the middle of the cage, was a very beautiful, very green, very soft-looking nest.

uh oh

She lifted up the top of the nest, and she

screamed,

'arcHHHH, BERNARD!!!'

He was lying on his back in the middle of the nest with his legs in the air, his little black eyes fixed and bulging, and his mouth, which was wide open, was full of very beautiful, very green, very expensive cashmere coat.

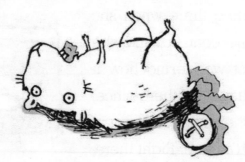

'And that,' said Nanna, 'was the end of Bernard. And *that* is why your Mum said she would "never, ever have another hamster". Because hamsters are all Bad News.'

And then Nanna gave us a kiss. Her kiss smelled like her talcum powder. And she turned out the light. And I stayed in Tom's bed because, like Nanna said, you don't have to stay in your own bed if it's the holidays.

CHAPTER 8
Ask And It Shall Be Given

Most of the time, if you ask Mum for something a lot, especially if you follow her around and do it in a voice that goes, '*Oh PLeeEAse, Mum... PLeeEAse...*' in the end she will say, 'Oh, for Goodness sake, alright.'

But not this time. Not with the hamster. Even with Tom asking, 'Why?'

And,

'What about if it's a very small hamster?'

Or,

'What about if we never let it out?'

Or,

'What about if we make it sleep in the garden?'

Mum just said, 'No' and put the hoover on, and turned the radio right up. So we decided to ask Suzanne to do a plan for getting a hamster with us.

We knocked on the wall three times and then we waited for a bit. Suzanne didn't knock back so either the coast wasn't clear, or she didn't hear us knocking because she was asleep, or maybe she was downstairs having her breakfast. So we knocked another three times, and waited again, and she still didn't knock back, so we knocked as hard as we could for a long time and then Suzanne's Dad opened the window very fast with his dressing gown on and he leaned out and shouted, **'FOR CRYING OUT LOUD, STOP BANGING ON THE WALL! AND RING ON THE DOORBELL LIKE A NORMAL HUMAN BEING!'**

I didn't want to ring on the doorbell like a normal human being so Tom went instead, and he told Suzanne we were doing a plan.

Suzanne came round, and she brought all her pens, and we made a new password for the day for Shed Club. It took quite a long time because Tom wanted the password to be 'Tom' and Suzanne said that was too easy.

And I wanted the password to be 'Hamster Plan' and Suzanne said if anyone heard it they would know that we were making a plan about a hamster.

And Suzanne wanted the password to be 'Rabbit', and I said the plan was about hamsters, not rabbits, so why should that be the password? But Suzanne said if the password wasn't 'Rabbit' she was going home, and she was taking her pens with her. So that was what it was.

After we decided on the password, Tom went in the house for a biscuit, and Suzanne started thinking of all the things that I could do to get a hamster. And I started writing them all down. We did two lists. And this is what they said…

ANNA'S AND SUZANNE'S TWO LISTS OF THINGS TO DO TO GET A HAMSTER

LIST NUMBER 1
Things To Do To Make Mum Let Us Have A Hamster

1. Jobs
2. Learn My Spellings
3. Cry
4. Go Back To Brownies And Say Sorry To Brown Owl
5. Stop Talking
6. Stop Eating

The thing was, I had already done most of the things that Suzanne thought of to put in List Number One. I had tried Jobs and I had tried to Learn My Spellings and I had tried Crying. Mum said I couldn't have a hamster but if I carried on crying she would give me an Oscar. And I was not going to go back to Brownies to say sorry to Brown Owl. I couldn't do that anyway, even if I wanted to, because Brown Owl said that I am Banned. And the only other things left on List Number One were Stop Eating, and Stop Talking, and I didn't think Mum would mind if I did either of those.

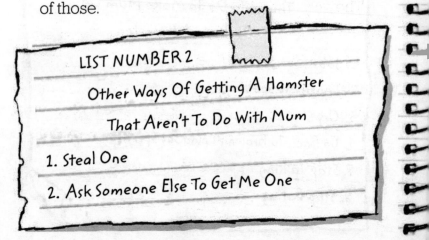

LIST NUMBER 2

Other Ways Of Getting A Hamster
That Aren't To Do With Mum

1. Steal One

2. Ask Someone Else To Get Me One

The first thing on List Number Two was steal a hamster. I didn't really want to steal anything again if I could help it because the last time I stole something Mum made me take it back, and she said she had half a mind to tell Nanna's friend Mrs Rotherham up the road on me because Mrs Rotherham used to be in the police. And then I would have to go to The Young Offenders' Institution, which is a jail, but for children, and I definitely wouldn't be allowed to have a hamster there. Me and Tom always used to run when we went past Mrs Rotherham's house.

The only other thing that was left on the list was to Ask Someone Else To Get Me One. Suzanne said I should ask My Dad. It's different with My Dad than Suzanne's Dad though, because if you ask My Dad something he never says 'Yes' or 'No',

51

he only says, 'Ask your mother. She's in charge.'

And then Mum says she is not in charge, and if she *was* in charge, Dad would be clearing out all of his rubbish from the cupboard under the stairs, like she has been asking him to do for the last ten years, instead of drinking beer and watching the football, and then she says, **'And NO. For the last time, you cannot have a hamster!'**

So we tried to think of someone else to ask to get me a hamster who was in charge of Mum. And the only person we could think of was Nanna.

Nanna stayed at our house a lot because of her hips, and needing help, and things like that. And some of the time when she came to our house she had to stay in bed. And then Nanna really liked it if we went into her room to ask her if she wanted anything. Normally she only wanted you to sit on the bed with her, which Mum said we could, as long as Nanna wasn't asleep. This time Nanna was asleep, but I went in to ask her if she wanted anything anyway because then I could ask her if she would get me a hamster. It took ages trying to ask Nanna because first she had to wake up, and then she had to put her hearing aid in, and then she couldn't turn it on, and it kept squeaking, and in the end she said I should just shout because she couldn't make the hearing aid work.

So I did. I tried shouting to ask if she wanted me to get her anything first, but she still couldn't hear, so in the end I just shouted as loud as I could, '*CAN. I. HAVE. A. HAMSTER?*'

Nanna laughed. I didn't laugh because I didn't think it was funny.

And then Nanna said, 'Ah, I'm sorry, Duck, hop up.' And she patted the bed. Nanna's bed smelled like her talcum powder. Nanna said, 'If I was in charge, I'd let you have ten hamsters, Duck. But I'm not, I'm sorry.'

And she cuddled me in, and stroked me on the head until she fell asleep again.

●ξ ●ξ ●ξ

I went back to the shed and told Suzanne what Nanna said about not being in charge. And I said that maybe we should go and dig up Joe-down-the-road's Old Rabbit instead, because none of the plans for getting a hamster were working. But Suzanne had thought of another person to ask for a hamster, someone who Mum wasn't in charge of, and that person was God.

CHAPTER 9
Our Father...

Sometimes, on Sundays, Mum and Nanna go to Church, and me and Tom go to Sunday School in the cottage next door to the Church, because children aren't allowed to be in Church for long in case they start laughing or crying or needing a wee. You can't do those kinds of things in Church. The only things you *can* do in Church are kneeling on the cushions and saying the Amens. Unless you are Confirmed, and then you can eat the Body Of Christ and drink His Blood.

But me and Tom aren't old enough to do that, so we go to Sunday School instead and just go into Church for the last bit at the end.

You can do most things in Sunday School, like colouring and singing and dressing up, as long as you don't dress up as Jesus on the cross, because Graham Roberts did that once, just in his pants, and Mrs Constantine didn't like it.

Mrs Constantine is in charge of Sunday School, and she is the Vicar's Wife.

Anyway, when Sunday School is finished you do the Prayer, and have a biscuit, and then everyone from Sunday School goes into Church for the last bit and sits with their Mums. Sometimes they sit with their Dads as well, but mostly they sit with their Mums because not many Dads go to Church.

Our Dad doesn't go. He doesn't even believe in God. Graham Roberts said Dad will probably go to Hell. Nanna said Dad won't go to Hell and Graham Roberts shouldn't say things like that because he doesn't know what he is talking about.

There aren't very many children in Sunday School. Sometimes it's ten, and sometimes it's six, and once it was only two, and that was when it was just me and Tom, and then Mrs Constantine said there wasn't any point in even doing Sunday School that week, and she made me and Tom go into Church for the whole time with Mum and Nanna. And that was when we got in Big Trouble because we had The Hysterics because first everyone in Church had to shake hands with each other and say, 'Peace be with you', and the lady who was sitting behind Tom kept saying 'Peath Be With You' instead. And then the Vicar said 'Hymn 97' and that's the hymn that goes…

> I was cold. I was naked.
> Were you there?
> Were you there?
> I was cold. I was naked.
> Were you there?

And me and Tom kept thinking about when Graham Roberts was Jesus, just in his pants. And then the lady who was sitting behind us who had said 'Peath Be With You' hit Tom hard on the head with her Hymn Book.

And then we *really* got The Hysterics. And we had to lie on the floor under the pew.

Nanna asked the Peath Be With You Lady if she would mind *not* hitting Tom on the head with her Hymn Book.

But the Peath Be With You Lady said she would very much mind not hitting Tom on the head with her Hymn Book, because Tom was Out Of Control and children like us had 'No buithneth being in Church'.

And Nanna said, 'Suffer the little children' which is something from in the Bible that Jesus said which means you can't really hit children on the head with your Hymn Book or anything, even if they *have* got The Hysterics.

The Peath Be With You Lady said, **'Thuffer nothing. They've ruined the thurvith.'**

And then Nanna had to leave the Church because she said she had a bad cough, but really it was because she had The Hysterics a bit too.

And she took me and Tom with her and we went to get an ice cream, even though it was raining, because Nanna said ice cream is good for calming down.

But we didn't get The Hysterics when we went to Church to ask God about having a hamster.

Mum didn't want to go to Church that day because Nanna was staying in bed with her hips. But we promised we wouldn't get The Hysterics and, in the end, Mum said 'alright then' because, when you ask to go to Church, it's not really the kind of thing that a Mum can say 'No' to. Not like when you ask to go to Alton Towers or something like that.

And Suzanne said she wanted to come along too

because she had never been to Church before.

In the morning, before we left, Mum said we should go and give Nanna a kiss and tell her we were going to Church because she would like that. Maybe she did like it but she didn't open her eyes. I gave Nanna a kiss on the cheek, and so did Suzanne, and Tom gave her a kiss on the hand because he doesn't like kissing Nanna on the cheek because he says she prickles, which she does, but only a little bit. Nanna's cheek smelled like her talcum powder. Suzanne said our Nanna looked very small in the bed, which she did, because she hardly made a shape under the covers, but the bed is quite big so that probably made her look smaller.

Mrs Constantine was pleased that we had brought a new person to Sunday School and she was even more pleased when she asked Suzanne what she would like to do and Suzanne said 'I need to ask God for something'.

Mrs Constantine told Suzanne that, 'asking God for something is called praying'. Which Suzanne already knew, but she pretended she didn't. Mrs Constantine gave Suzanne a Bible, and she showed her which page told you how to do praying. It was quite hard to read, so Mrs Constantine read it first. She said,'But thou, when thou prayest, enter into thy closet, and when thou hast shut thy door, pray to thy Father which is in secret; and thy Father which seeth in secret shall reward thee openly. . . After this manner therefore pray ye:

Our Father which art in heaven,
Hallowed be thy name.
Thy kingdom come.
Thy will be done, In earth, as it is in heaven.
Give us this day our daily bread.
And forgive us our trespasses,
As we forgive those who trespass against us.
Lead us not into temptation,
But deliver us from evil:
For thine is the kingdom,
The power and the glory,
For ever and ever.
A-men.'

Suzanne said, 'Thank you' to Mrs Constantine, and she took the Bible.

We waited until Mrs Constantine wasn't looking, and then me and Tom and Suzanne snuck up the stairs, where you aren't supposed to go, into the store room where there is a big cupboard, which is almost a closet, where all the old Bibles are, and the Hymn Books, and the purple cloths, and the gold crosses and things like that, because that was the best place to do it.

It was pretty dark inside the old cupboard, once you got right in. I wanted Suzanne and Tom to come in the cupboard with me, but Suzanne said I had to go in on my own and close the door, and pray in secret like Mrs Constantine said.

I said the Prayer, the bits I could remember, because it was too dark to read, and then I said, 'Amen', and then I waited for a bit. And then, just to make sure, I said, 'Can I have a hamster?'

And then I said 'Please.'

And then I said 'Amen', again.

When I was finished, and I tried to get out of the cupboard, I couldn't find the door because it was too dark and I couldn't remember which side of the cupboard it was on. I shouted for Tom and Suzanne but they had gone back downstairs to do singing with the others. Tom always sings the loudest even though he doesn't know the words. I pushed, but the door didn't open. The cupboard was very dark and it smelled dusty, of old things and mothballs, like Nanna's house used to. And I could smell Nanna's talcum powder, as strong as if Nanna was there in the cupboard too.

I breathed in the smell as much as I could, until I thought I was going to sneeze, and I shouted,

'LET ME OUT!'

And then a spider, or a mouse, or a rat ran over my foot. So then I *really* wanted to get out of the cupboard. I am not scared of spiders and mice and rats and things because I quite like them, but I don't really like them running over my feet in a dark cupboard when I can't see. So I leaned on the door as hard as I could, and I screamed,

'HELP!'

And then the whole cupboard fell right over, and it crashed onto the floor with me inside.

Mrs Constantine ran upstairs and said 'Hello? Who's there?

And I said 'Me.'

And she said 'Who?'

And I said,

'ME! HELP! I'M IN THE CUPBOARD.'

But Mrs Constantine couldn't help because she couldn't lift the cupboard up because it was quite a heavy cupboard, even when I wasn't inside it, and I weigh five stones and two pounds, which is 28 kilograms, so she had to get the caretaker.

When I got out we all had a biscuit, and some juice, and looked for the rat, but we couldn't find

it because it had got away, and then we went into Church for the last bit. And we stood at the back. And the Vicar said, 'Therefore I say unto you, what things soever ye desire, when ye pray, believe that ye receive them, and ye shall have them. For everyone that asketh receiveth; and he that seeketh findeth; and to him that knocketh it shall be opened. Or what man is there of you, whom if his son ask bread, will he give him a stone? Or if he ask a fish, will he give him a serpent?'

And Suzanne whispered, 'Or, if she ask for a hamster, will he give a rat?'

And Mrs Constantine said, 'Shh.'

And then we went to sit with Mum.

👣 👣 👣

When we got home, Dad told me and Tom to wait downstairs while Mum went upstairs to see

Nanna, but Tom went up anyway, and I followed after.

Mum was sitting on Nanna's bed. And Nanna was in it. Nanna looked even smaller in the bed than before. And Mum was crying.

Tom asked Mum if she was sad. Mum nodded her head.

Tom said, 'Why?' But Mum didn't answer because she put her hand over her mouth instead. And she patted the bed with her other hand.

And me and Tom got up. I could smell Nanna's talcum powder again. And Mum said that Nanna was dead. And she cried for a long time then, and she cuddled us in, and she stroked us on the head.

CHAPTER 10

The Hamsters Came In Two By Two

After Nanna died, I decided I wouldn't ask Mum about a hamster again, and I wouldn't tell her how Nanna said if she was in charge she would let me have ten hamsters, or how I asked God for one, because Mum was sad quite a lot.

Then, the day after Nanna's funeral, Mum said we were going to a special shop.

Tom said, 'Has it got hamsters?'

And Mum said, 'Yes.'

The man in the shop had a brand new kind of hamster

cage that was round and made of plastic, and it had plastic tubes to go with it, which you could attach together to make tunnels. And the Pet Shop Man said that was the best kind of hamster cage you could get.

But Mum said we had only come in the shop to get one normal hamster, and she had already agreed to buy two Russian Dwarf hamsters, and an exercise-wheel, and a water bottle, and a book called *Hamsters: A Manual*. And we had a perfectly good cage at home in the cupboard under the stairs and Dad would just have to find it.

So the Pet Shop Man put the hamsters in a brown box with some sawdust and some air holes and we took the hamsters home in that.

◦⁝ ◦⁝ ◦⁝

When we got to the bottom of our road, Tom ran ahead to see if Dad had found the cage yet. Mr Tucker was in the road picking up litter, which he always does. And Tom was running up the road, and Mr Tucker was coming out of the hedge backwards, and he had some toilet paper in one hand, and a bin bag full of litter in his other hand, and there were lots of sticky-buds and twigs and things stuck to his tie and his blazer. And Tom was running his fastest, and he probably had his eyes shut, and Mr Tucker looked up and saw Tom coming and he said, 'Hallo, look keen! Let up!'

But Tom ran right into Mr Tucker, and Mr Tucker dropped the toilet paper and the bin bag full of litter and said, 'Oomph! Good God! What a belt!'

And Tom fell over on the gravel.

And Mr Tucker said, 'What's this arrival, eh? I could have done with an Arse-end Charlie there. I think that makes you an Ace, old chum.'

And Tom started crying.

And Mr Tucker said, 'Ah ha, frozen on the stick, eh? Well, where's your salute, Sir? You know the drill. On your feet. Look lively. Fling one up.'

And Tom got up and gave Mr Tucker the salute, even though he was crying, because it's one of Tom's best things to do when he sees Mr Tucker, and Mr Tucker gave him one back and he said, 'Smashing job. Good show, me old sawn-off. Where's that knee? Better have a quick shufti. Ooh, a humdinger. Dicey do, that was. You'll live, I'd say, but will you have to have the leg off?

73

What do you think?'

And Tom said, 'No', because he had stopped crying, and his knee was only bleeding a bit.

And Mr Tucker said, 'No? Quite right. That's the spirit. Press on regardless. You're not washed out yet. Plane's a write-off but you'll just have to wear it. Be glad you didn't land in the drink. In a bad way myself, as it goes. Got me in the goolies.'

And that made Tom laugh.

And Mr Tucker said, 'Hallo' to Mum.

And Mum said, 'Hello' to Mr Tucker.

And I didn't say anything because I didn't want to start talking to Mr Tucker in case it was about litter.

And then Mr Tucker said to Mum, 'Black do, your mother hopping the twig. Heard a buzz the old girl was low on juice. Clocked the blood wagon outside a week gone Sunday, thought "Hallo, look up," and a couple of body-snatchers bringing her in. Bad show all round. Beautiful blonde job like that. Doesn't do. Doesn't do.'

And Mum said, 'Thank you.'

And then Mr Tucker said, 'What do you say, Popsie? She was a fine woman, eh?'

And I said, 'Yes.'

And Mr Tucker said, 'A very fine woman.' And then he said, 'And she was flat out for me plugging away at this litter situation. Took a dim view of it, very dim, I can tell you. Last time I saw her she said to me, "Wing Commander", she said, "I think somebody, somewhere, is playing silly beggars with this litter." "Silly beggars," she said.'

And then Mr Tucker stared at me until Tom said, 'We've got hamsters.'

Mr Tucker pointed his finger at me, and closed one eye and said, 'Mmmmm.'

I didn't say anything to Mr Tucker but I don't

76

believe Nanna said anything about silly beggars because for one thing that wasn't really the kind of thing that Nanna did say, and if she *was* going to say it, she probably wouldn't say it to Mr Tucker because she didn't like talking about litter much either.

Mr Tucker said, 'Hamsters, Tom, is it? Where d'you get 'em?'

And Tom said, 'The pet shop.'

And Mr Tucker said, 'Pet shop, eh?'

And Tom said, 'Yes.'

And Mr Tucker said, 'How many?'

And Tom said, 'Two.'

Mr Tucker said, 'Two of 'em, eh?'

And Tom said, 'Yes.'

And Mr Tucker said, 'Smashing.'

And Tom said, 'Yes.'

And I was getting bored of listening to Tom and Mr Tucker so I said, 'They're from Russia.'

RUSSIA
Россия

Mr Tucker said, 'Russia? Good God, Girl! Have you lost your wool completely?'

And I said how the man in the shop said that the Russian ones were the best.

Mr Tucker said, 'I'd take a lean view of that, my girl. I know a thing or two about the Russians. Slippery. Very slippery.'

And then Mr Tucker took the box with the hamsters in off me, and took the lid off, and the hamsters could have got out or anything.

But they didn't.

And Mr Tucker looked in the box and he said, 'Just as I thought. Couple of gremlins. What are you calling them?'

Tom said, 'Don't know.'

And Mr Tucker said, 'Number One, and Number Two, Basher. That's what I'd call 'em.'

And Tom said, 'I need a wee.'

Which he did because he was hopping from one foot to the other, and he had been doing it for ages, and that's what he does when he needs a wee.

So Mr Tucker gave Tom the salute.

And Tom gave Mr Tucker the salute back.

And Mr Tucker said, 'That's it. You've got the green, Old Chum. Chocks away.'

And then he made Tom's hair messy.

And then he looked at me and said, 'Silly

beggars… Mmmm.'

And then he went back into the hedge.

And me and Tom and Mum went into the house.

CHAPTER 11
Housing The Hamsters

When we got in the house Dad had found the hamster cage and he'd cleaned it out, and put it in my room, and put some sawdust in it, and a food bowl. And Mum attached the water bottle and then she put the wheel in. The only thing with the hamsters was, because of them being Russian Dwarf hamsters, when we put them in the cage, their legs were too small to make the wheel go round, and their mouths were too small to get the water out of the bottle, and their bodies were too small to not be able to get out between the

bars. And they did get out between the bars. And one of them weed on the carpet. And Mum started crying, and left the room, even though it was only a little wee. But Dad said Mum wasn't really crying about the wee, and not to worry.

Tom said, 'Is she crying about Nanna?'

And Dad said, 'Yes.'

And then Mum and Dad went into Nanna's room, and closed the door, and they changed Nanna's bed, and put her things in boxes. And afterwards it looked like nothing had ever happened.

Me and Tom cleaned up the wee on the carpet and we put the hamsters back in the brown box with the air-holes. And after that Mum went to bed.

Then Dad went to see Mrs Rotherham up

the road because she has got a lot of fish in her house, and he said maybe she had an old fish tank that we could borrow, and we could use that for a hamster cage instead. And Tom stayed in the house because he didn't want to go to Mrs Rotherham's because Mrs Rotherham used to be in the police, and Mum sometimes said she had half a mind to tell Mrs Rotherham on Tom when he was In Trouble, and Tom wasn't sure if she had or not. And I stayed in the house too because I needed to find out some things about the hamsters.

CHAPTER 12

From Russia With Love

This is what it said in my dictionary about Russians...

Russian [rush-un] ✦ *noun*
someone or something from Russia

And this is what it said in my dictionary about dwarfs...

dwarf [dworf] ✦ *noun*
a person of abnormally small stature
suffering from a bone growth disorder

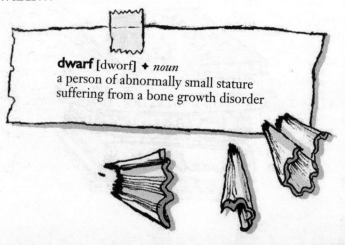

I didn't think that the hamsters were suffering from anything, except maybe being in the box, so I went and knocked on Suzanne's wall to see what the dictionary said in her house. Suzanne isn't allowed to take the dictionary out of her house anymore because last time she took it, when we needed to look up some words from Joe-down-the-road's Mum's book in the shed, she forgot to take it back. And that was when I thought it would be a good lid for the worms.

It wasn't a very good lid for the worms because the next day the worms weren't really moving anymore. And then the dictionary got some of the worms' mud on it. And then Suzanne got in Big Trouble off her Dad, because he said, **'WHERE ON EARTH IS MY DICTIONARY, SUZANNE?'**

And Suzanne came to my house to get it, and we tried to get the mud off but it just made it worse, and then Mum said I had to go with Suzanne to take the dictionary back.

And then Suzanne's Dad said, **'WHAT IN GOD'S NAME HAVE YOU BEEN DOING WITH IT?'**

And I said about how I had been using it for a worm lid.

And Suzanne's Dad said, **'DOES IT *LOOK* LIKE A**

WORM LID, FOR CRYING OUT LOUD?'

And then Suzanne's Dad said Suzanne was never allowed to take the dictionary, or anything else, out of his house again, because of Suzanne being,

'...INCAPABLE OF BEHAVING LIKE A NORMAL HUMAN BEING!'

I said that maybe Suzanne could go and get the dictionary anyway, because her Dad wasn't at home, and she could stay in her room with the dictionary, which wouldn't be taking it out of the house, and I could go on the window ledge, and she could read what it says about dwarfs through the window and I could write it down, and then she could put the dictionary straight back.

So that is what we did.

This is what it said about dwarfs in the dictionary in Suzanne's house…

dwarf [dworf] ✦ *noun*
a being in the form of a small mythical man, usually having magic powers

I didn't think the hamsters were men, because Mum asked the Pet Shop Man about ten times, and the Pet Shop Man said they were definitely both female. And I didn't think they had magic powers because I don't believe in that kind of thing anymore, because I am nine. Anyway, then the dictionary in Suzanne's house said…

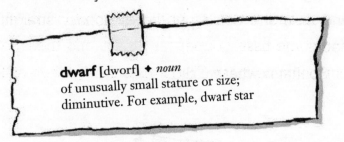

dwarf [dworf] ✦ *noun*
of unusually small stature or size; diminutive. For example, dwarf star

The hamsters *were* unusually small, because that was how they got through the bars in the cage. Suzanne said she knew how to spot Dwarf Stars, and she said she would tell me all about them if I liked. But I said I had to go and check on the hamsters. And then Suzanne said she had got a new bike that used to be her cousin's, and I should come to her house and see it. But Dad came back with a new wheel that was smaller, and a water bowl, and a fish tank from Mrs Rotherham. So I said, 'I'll knock for you later' and I shut the window.

●: ●: ●:

We put the sawdust in the fish tank, and the new wheel, and the water bowl, and the food bowl, and some tissue paper for a nest, and then we put the hamsters in. The hamsters stood very still in the middle of the fish tank. And then we looked in the book for what to do next. And Dad read it with us because it was quite hard to read.

"The Russian Dwarf, or Djungarian, Hamster, properly known as Phodopus Sungoris Campbelli and otherwise referred to as Campbell's Dwarf Hamster, or Hairy-Footed Dwarf Hamster, ought not to be confused with the Winter White, or Siberian, Hamster from the closely-related sub-species, Phodopus Sungorus."

Tom said he didn't like the book and he wanted to go and see Mum.

But Dad said he couldn't, and he gave Tom a whole packet of biscuits, chocolate ones, and then Tom said he didn't mind staying. So Dad read some more.

"The Russian Dwarf Hamster is a diminutive rodent, compact of body, with an undersized tail and, in common with all Cricetinae, expandable cheek pouches. The range of normal length of the Russian Dwarf lies between 60 and 113 millimetres (tail inclusive)."

We got a tape measure, and we measured the hamsters, which was quite hard because they didn't really like being measured. Hamster Number One was 56 millimetres long, and its tail was seven millimetres. And she was the Small One. Hamster Number Two was 62 millimetres long, and I couldn't measure its tail because it kept trying to bite me. But she was the Big One.

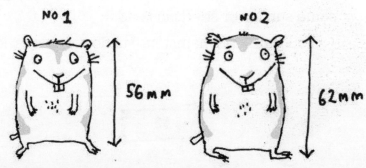

Anyway, then it said in the book…

"There are numerous variants and hybrids in terms of coat and colouring. Most commonly, the fur of the upper body is short, flat and greyish brown, with a white underside, and a dark brown stripe running the length of the spine. Such a variant is found in the wild, as well as domestically, and is properly referred to as the Agouti."

I didn't want to read the book anymore because it was hard to understand, and it didn't really help with what to do with hamsters, and Tom didn't want to read the book anymore either because he had finished the biscuits. So Dad went to go and find something to make a lid for the fish tank. And me and Tom gave the hamsters some sunflower seeds instead.

You can feed hamsters sunflower seeds for

ages because they just keep taking more and more and they stuff them in their cheeks until they look like they are going to burst and then (which is my best bit) they go into a corner and they push all the seeds out of their cheeks, and they bury them in the sawdust for eating later.

If you want, you can collect up the old seeds that have been in their cheeks after they've emptied them out, and you can give them back to the hamsters to put them in their cheeks again, and that means you don't have to buy millions of seeds all the time. It's not very nice when you put the old seeds back in because they're normally pretty soggy, and sometimes they're mixed in with other things they've put in their cheeks, and sometimes that can be poos.

I put some of the sunflower seeds on my hands and on my arms. And Hamster Number Two, which was the Big One, crawled along and put them in her cheeks. And then I put some sunflower seeds on Tom's arms, and on his shoulders, and some on the top of his head and Hamster Number Two ran all over him.

Tom didn't really like that, because Hamster Number Two was too fast, and he didn't like its feet, and it emptied all the soggy sunflower seeds out of its cheeks in Tom's hair. Tom said he liked Hamster Number One better because it was smaller and because it would sit still in your hand if you were very quiet, and it didn't mind being stroked if you gave it the crumbs from the biscuits.

And then the doorbell rang and it was Suzanne. I knew it was Suzanne because she did three rings. So I put the hamsters back in the fish-tank and I told Tom to watch them, and I went to the door.

Suzanne said, 'Are you coming out?'

And I said, 'No. I need to make an obstacle course for the hamsters. You could come in.'

But Suzanne said, 'No. I need to go on my bike. It's new.'

And I said, 'You can hold one of the hamsters.'

But Suzanne said, 'No. I don't want to. I'm probably allergic.'

I said, 'No, you're not.'

And Suzanne said, 'I could be. My Dad is. It might run in families.'

And I said, 'You're Dad's probably not allergic.

95

He's probably lying.'

And Suzanne said, 'My Dad's not a liar. *You're* a liar. You said you were going to knock on the wall for me later and you didn't.'

And then she said she was going to tell her Dad about how I made her get the dictionary. And she said she was going to call on Joe-down-the-road and ask him to come and play on bikes instead.

And I said, 'Good.' Because I said she probably loved Joe-down-the-road, and she was probably going to do all the things from Joe's Mum's book.

And Suzanne said, 'No. You are, and you've probably done them already.' And then she got on her bike and went away.

Sometimes I hate Suzanne.

I started doing the obstacle course and everything and then Suzanne came round to the back door. I knew it was Suzanne because she did three knocks.

When I opened the back door it was very loud because the bin lorry was there, collecting the rubbish. And Suzanne had to shout. She said, 'DO YOU WANT TO GO IN THE SHED AND MAKE A PLAN FOR DIGGING UP THE OLD RABBIT AND EVERYTHING AND I CAN BRING ALL MY PENS OVER AND CARD AND THINGS AND WE CAN MAKE A BOX?'

And I said, 'NO.' Because I was too busy with the hamsters.

And Suzanne said, 'DO YOU WANT TO LOOK AT MY BIKE?'

And I said, 'WHAT?' Because the Bin Lorry was getting louder because it was right by

Suzanne's back door.

And Suzanne said, 'MY BIKE!'

And I said, 'WHERE IS IT?'

And Suzanne said, 'THERE.'

And I said, 'WHERE?'

And Suzanne said, 'THERE! BY THE BINS!'

And she turned round and pointed to the bins. But her bike *wasn't* there because one of its wheels was sticking out of the bin lorry.

SUZANNE'S BIKE

And Suzanne screamed and ran to the Bin Man and said, **'GET IT OUT! THAT'S MY NEW BIKE!'**

But the teeth came down. There was a big crunch and a grinding noise.

And the Bin Man said, **'TOO LATE, LOVE. I'M NOT PSYCHIC! IF IT'S NOT FOR THE BIN LORRY, DON'T PUT IT BY THE BINS!'**

And he got in the bin lorry and drove off.

And Suzanne ran home.

And there was a lot of shouting in Suzanne's house because we heard it through the wall. And Suzanne cried a lot. Because of the bike. And the Bin Man. And her Dad. And because it wasn't her fault really.

And then, when it went quiet, she knocked on my wall three times.

And I opened my window.

And Suzanne opened her window and she said, 'I hate you.' And then she shut her window.

I didn't shut mine. I stayed on the window ledge for ages. There was a magpie in the garden, and I wanted to tell Suzanne because Nanna once told me and Suzanne that whenever you see a magpie you should always say, 'Hello, Mr Magpie. How's your wife and children?' because that stops you getting bad luck. And, since then, we always do. So I knocked on Suzanne's window. But Suzanne closed her curtains.

When I came in from the window ledge the New Cat was in my bedroom. It was crouched very low down. And its eyes were very wide. And its mouth was very open. And it was staring right at the hamsters.

❝ CHAPTER 13 ❞
The Birds And The Bees

Tom didn't look after the hamsters as much as me because sometimes he wanted to go outside and do other things, like hold the bin bag for the litter for Mr Tucker, or walk in a straight line with his eyes closed, or collect gravel. But I didn't want to go out at all because I didn't feel like it, and because Suzanne didn't want to be my friend anymore, and because if Suzanne decided she *did* want to be my friend again I knew that she would knock on the wall and, if I went out, I wouldn't hear her. So I stayed in my room on my own with the hamsters. And that's probably why I didn't notice that anything was different about

Number One. Because you don't really know that something is growing if you see it a lot. And that's why when you see a grown-up that you haven't seen for ages they say, 'Ooh, you've grown' but people who see you every day, like your Mum, don't say it because it happens too slowly for them to notice.

Tom said, 'Number One is fat.'

'No she isn't,' I said.

'Yes she is,' Tom said. 'She's fat. She's more fatter than Number Two.'

I looked at Number One, and I looked at Number Two. And Number One *was* fatter. A lot fatter.

'She used to be more skinnier,' Tom said.

I measured Number Two's tummy. She bit me. It was 76 millimetres around. And then I measured

Number One's tummy. It was 109 mm around. I decided to put Number One on a diet.

It was quite hard putting Number One on a diet because Number One and Number Two shared the same food bowl. So I took Number One out of the fish-tank when I fed Number Two. And I took Number Two out when I fed Number One. And I did that with gardening gloves on because of Number Two's biting.

I gave Number One half the amount of food that I gave Number Two. And I didn't give Number One any sunflower seeds. And I made sure that Number Two didn't put her sunflower seeds in her cheeks to hide for later, in case Number One found them and ate them all. Because even though *I* wouldn't eat something that had been in someone else's cheeks and spat back out again, hamsters aren't very fussy about things like that.

I measured Number One every day. But she didn't get any smaller. She just kept on getting bigger.

One afternoon Mum came into my room and Tom said, 'Number One is fat and she's getting even fatter. She's going to pop.'

Mum looked at Number One and she said, 'Oh, please God, no.' And she went downstairs to phone the Pet Shop Man.

Me and Tom picked up the other phone in Mum's room and listened in. We aren't allowed to listen in on the other phone, because Mum says it's rude, but sometimes we have to if it's very important.

Mum said, 'I think one of the hamsters you sold us is pregnant.'

Tom said, 'Oh!'

Mum said, 'Anna and Tom, I know you're there. Put the phone down.'

We put the phone down. It was hard to be quiet because if Number One *was* pregnant that meant we would get a baby hamster.

In fact that meant we would get *lots* of baby hamsters because hamsters don't just have one or two or even three babies at a time like people do. They have six, or seven, or eight, or something like that. And one hamster, who lived in Louisiana, in America, had 26 babies at a time, and that hamster got in the book of *Guinness World Records*.

We picked the other phone up again to listen.

The Pet Shop Man said, 'She can't be pregnant because both the hamsters I sold you are female.'

Mum said, 'Maybe it was pregnant before it left the shop.'

The Pet Shop Man said, 'No. Impossible. It was only three weeks old, and every single hamster in this shop is female.'

Mum said, 'Well, what are you suggesting, an immaculate conception?'

I know all about what an immaculate conception is because I was the Angel Gabriel in the Nativity at Church last year, and I had to visit Mary to tell her she was going to have a baby, and when Mary said to me, 'How shall this be, seeing that I know not a man?' I had to say, 'The Holy Ghost shall come upon thee, and the power of the Highest shall overshadow thee: therefore also that holy thing which shall be born of thee shall be called the Son of God. For with God nothing shall be impossible.'

And that's what an immaculate conception is. But it doesn't happen with hamsters because I don't think it ever even happens with people, apart from Mary. Maybe.

Anyway, the Pet Shop Man said, 'Maybe your hamster has just got wind.'

And Mum said, 'It's been getting fatter for weeks.'

And the Pet Shop man said, 'Or it could be a Phantom Pregnancy.'

And I said, 'What's a Phantom Pregnancy?'

And Mum said,

'PUT THE PHONE DOWN!'

And then she said, 'How do I check if the other hamster is male?'

And the Pet Shop Man told her how.

Mum put the phone down. And me and Tom put the other phone down. And we ran back into my room and we sat on the bed.

Mum came in, and she picked Number Two

up, and she turned Number Two on her back to look at her tummy. Number Two didn't like being on her back, and she bit Mum, and then Mum dropped Number Two, and she couldn't catch her for ages, and each time she did catch her, Number Two bit her again.

I got the gardening gloves and I put Number Two back in the fish-tank. Mum said she would look at Number Two again tomorrow when she could take her by surprise.

I asked Mum what a Phantom Pregnancy was again.

Mum said, 'It's nothing, Big Ears. It's time for bed.'

It didn't sound like nothing to me. It didn't have Phantom Pregnancy in the dictionary in my house, but it did have Phantom, and it didn't sound very good.

This is what it said...

phantom [fan-tum] ✦ *noun*
a spirit of a dead person believed by
some to visit the living as a pale, almost
transparent form of a person, animal or
other object; a ghost

I wanted to knock on the wall to ask Suzanne
what it said in the dictionary in her house about
phantoms, in case the ones in my dictionary
weren't the right kind. But I knew Suzanne
wouldn't knock back. So I went to bed instead.

I had a dream. A bad one. About Nanna. She was
in the back lane, and she was see-through, like
a phantom, and she was digging in the ground
trying to find the Old Rabbit. When I woke up it

was still dark. I looked at my clock. It was 2.00 a.m. That means it was two o'clock in the morning. I've got a digital clock because I'm not very good with the time.

Anyway, it was the middle of the night, and the hamster wheel was squeaking. I took the lid off the fish-tank. Hamster Number Two was on the wheel. I pulled back some of the tissue paper from the top of the nest to see if Number One was in there. And she was. And next to Number One was a pale pink see-through thing that was moving. And when I looked closer it wasn't *one*

pale pink see-through thing that was moving, it was *lots* of little pale pink see-through things.

They were tiny, like small prawns, and you could see all their veins, and you could even see their hearts beating through their skin. At first I thought they must be phantoms like the Pet Shop Man said, and like it said in the dictionary, but then I looked in the Hamster Manual.

I couldn't really understand what it said about baby hamsters because of it using lots of hard words, but it had a picture of some babies, and they looked exactly like the Phantom Hamsters in the fish-tank. So I decided they probably weren't Phantom Hamsters after all, even though they looked all pale and everything, because that's how they looked in the book too, and anyway when Tom was born he looked a bit pale and see-through too and *he* wasn't a phantom.

I went into Tom's room and woke him up and he came to see.

'Oh, look!' he said, 'There's millions of them.' And he laughed, and then he hopped about from one foot to the other like he does when he needs a wee, but faster. And I did it too because that's the dance that me and Tom do sometimes, when something we love happens.

Tom said, 'Count them. Count them!'

I counted the babies and there were eight. And then me and Tom got The Hysterics a bit, and we had to put our heads under the duvet so we didn't wake Mum up. And we had The Hysterics for ages. Because now we had eight new Baby Hamsters, and soon their eyes would open, and they would stop looking like phantoms,

113

and start growing, and getting fur, and running around. And we would have ten hamsters altogether, and they could all do the obstacle course. And because as soon as we could tell them apart we would have to think of eight names for the new ones. And because we would never have been allowed eight more hamsters if we had asked but now that we had them, no one could take them away because they would have to stay with their mum until they were all grown-up.

I put the lid back on the fish-tank. Or at least I meant to put the lid back on the fish-tank. And I shut my bedroom door. Or at least I meant to shut my bedroom door. And Tom got in my bed, because I didn't feel like sleeping on my own very much. And we talked about the Baby Hamsters, and what we might call them. And then we fell asleep.

And when I woke up it was because Tom said, 'Ugh!'

CHAPTER 14
The Hamster MASSACRE

'Look,' Tom said. He pointed at the fish-tank.

There were spots on the glass. And the sawdust near the nest was wet. I lifted up the tissue paper. It was sticky and red. And underneath, in the middle, were the eight Baby Hamsters. They were covered in blood. And all of them were dead. Number One was in the corner of the tank. She had blood around her mouth, and one of her back legs had gone. And the other thing that had gone was Hamster Number Two.

'There's only one hamster left,' Tom said.

And I said, 'MUUUUUUUUUUM!'

❝ CHAPTER 15 ❞

In Shock

The Vet put three stitches in the end of the stump where Number One's back foot used to be. Number One didn't move, and she didn't even squeak. The Vet said she thought that Number One was in shock. And I said I thought Number One was in shock too, because I would be in shock if something bit my back leg off and killed all my babies and kidnapped my friend.

But The Vet said, 'I'm afraid to say this hamster probably killed the babies herself. It's quite common. You see, the male hamster becomes more and more aggressive during the pregnancy, and the female feels threatened, and

eliminates her dependants. You weren't to know, but it's a standard response. I'm very sorry.'

I didn't really know what eliminates or dependants or standard was, but I said that one thing I *did* know was that Number One wouldn't kill her own babies, even if she did feel threatened, because she wasn't really that kind of hamster. And I also knew for another thing that Number Two wasn't a male hamster because the Pet Shop Man had said she was a female.

The Vet said, 'Mmm, the Pet Shop Man. How long have you had the hamsters?'

And I said, 'five weeks.'

And The Vet said, 'Well, there you are, you see. The gestation period of a hamster, which is to say the time from conception to birth, is around twenty-one days.'

I didn't say anything.

The Vet said, 'How old are you?'

I didn't see what how old I was had to do with anything but I said, 'I am nine' anyway, and The Vet said, 'How can I put it? Urm… It's like this. A girl buys two hamsters. She has had the hamsters for five weeks when one of the hamsters gives birth. The length of time for which hamsters are pregnant is around three weeks. Did the hamster become pregnant before or after the girl bought it? And, if the hamster became pregnant *after* the girl bought it, what sex was the other hamster?'

I looked at my trainers because I hate sums

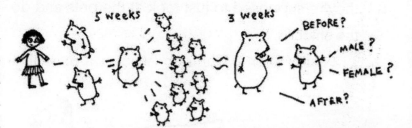

and I hate riddles, and I especially hate it when someone is staring at you and waiting for you to answer because it stops you being able to think, so I undid the laces on my trainers. And then I did them back up again.

And Mum said, 'You see? Unless it *was* an immaculate conception.'

I said, 'No. It wasn't an immaculate conception because hamsters don't have immaculate conceptions because that only happened to Mary.'

And then The Vet laughed. Even though it wasn't funny and even though vets aren't supposed to ask people sums or riddles or laugh at jokes or anything like that because they're supposed to just look at the pets and do the stitches.

I said, 'Even if Number Two *was* a male that

doesn't mean it was him who bit Number One's leg off, because it could have been something else. Because anyone could have got in the fish-tank and taken Number Two away and bitten Number One's leg off and killed the babies.'

And Mum said, 'Like who?'

And I said, 'Like the New Cat.'

And The Vet said, 'This wound is not consistent with something that might be inflicted by a cat, I'm afraid. Also, a cat would not leave Hamster Number One alive, and it would not cover the Baby Hamsters over, and leave them dead in the nest. Cats take their kills away with them, you see.'

I didn't say anything because The Vet didn't know what the New Cat was like. Because the New Cat didn't just bite things, sometimes she killed things by scaring them to death and things like that. Like with the Old Rabbit. And foxes sometimes kill chickens and just leave them. Graham Roberts told me that, and his Dad is a farmer, and they know more about things killing things than vets do.

I said, 'Well, where is Number Two now?'

And The Vet said, 'That is the question. It must have escaped.'

But I didn't think that Number Two had escaped because, even though I might have forgotten to put the lid on the fish-tank, and even though I might have left my bedroom door open, Number Two couldn't climb up the glass. Not unless it got on top of the wheel. And Number Two had only ever got on top of the wheel once before because it was a very hard thing to do.

Anyway, I didn't speak to The Vet after that because she said that she didn't think that Number One would live very long without her leg. And I wanted to go home.

●⦙ ●⦙ ●⦙

When we got back to the house I went upstairs to have a look at the dead Baby Hamsters. But the dead Baby Hamsters weren't there because Dad had cleaned the fish-tank out, and he had put new sawdust in, and he had made it look like nothing had ever even happened. Just like in Nanna's room. And he had got all the old sawdust, and the nest with the blood, and all the Baby Hamsters, and put them in a carrier bag. And he had put the carrier bag in the outside bin.

123

I ran out the back. Dad shouted after me, and Mum grabbed me by my hood, but I wriggled out of my coat, and I got away, and I got the carrier bag out of the bin, and Dad said, 'Put it back.'

And I said,

'THEY DON'T GO IN THE BIN!'

And I ran past Mum and Dad and upstairs to my room, and I shut the door, and sat against it. And Mum and Dad and Tom wanted to come in but I didn't let them because Dad had put the hamsters in the bin, and Mum didn't even want the hamsters in the first place, and Tom said 'Ugh' about the babies.

And I sat against the door until they all went away. And then I looked inside the carrier bag. I took out the nest, and I picked the eight Baby Hamsters out, one by one, and they were cold, and wet, and I put them on some tissue in my sandwich box. And then I put the lid on the box. And then I cried. And I couldn't stop crying. And I didn't want to.

After ages I heard three knocks on the wall. I stopped crying and I went to my window and I opened it. Suzanne opened her window too. She got out on the window ledge. 'I heard about your hamsters,' she said.

I said, 'Number Two has gone missing and Number One has only got three legs left and she had to have stitches and she had eight babies and they're all dead and Dad put them in the bin and I got them out.'

Suzanne said 'Can I see?'

So I lifted up the lid on the sandwich box and showed her the eight tiny hamsters in a row on the tissue.

Suzanne said, 'They don't look like hamsters.'

Because they didn't really.

I said, 'It's because they are a bit mushed and they haven't got their fur yet.' And then I put the lid back on the hamsters and I started crying again because they never would get any fur because they were dead, and because they were so small, and because they hadn't even opened their eyes yet, and because Dad put them in the bin, and because I didn't want Number Two to have bitten Number One's leg off and escaped, and because I didn't want Number One to have killed all the babies.

But Suzanne said, 'Maybe it wasn't Number Two who bit Number One's leg off, and maybe it wasn't Number One who killed the babies because maybe it was someone else, and maybe you are right about the New Cat, or the fox, and maybe we could find out what really happened and who really killed the hamsters because we could do an investigation!'

And then Suzanne said she would help me to do an investigation. And she would help me to bury the Baby Hamsters too, if I liked.

I said, 'I haven't got anything little enough to bury them in.'

But Suzanne said that she did. And she said she would bring all the things that we needed for burying the hamsters over to the shed.

And then she said, 'You can choose the password.'

I said, 'The password should be Dead.'

And Suzanne said, 'Yes.'

CHAPTER 16
Ashes To Ashes

Suzanne brought eight matchboxes. And she brought coloured paper. And all her pens. And glue. And glitter. And her best shells from the beach to stick on the boxes. And she brought some twigs and some twine to make crosses. And a shoebox that she had covered in black paper with red ribbon to put around it.

'It's for the Old Rabbit,' she said. Because if I didn't mind, she said, we could dig the Old Rabbit up and bury it again at the same time as the hamsters. And I didn't mind. So that is what we decided to do.

We stayed in the shed making the boxes for the Baby Hamsters all day, and we did them in eight different colours, and Mum brought us some sandwiches, and we didn't even come out for lunch, and we stuck a shell on each one, and some glitter, and we put a little bit of grass in them to make it nice inside.

When they were all done, I opened the lid of the sandwich box with the dead Baby Hamsters in, and I took the Baby Hamsters out one at a time, and I picked the sawdust off them, and the tissue paper, and Suzanne wiped the blood with her hankie. And I put each one in its own box. And I made eight holes in the ground next to where the Old Cat was buried, and Suzanne put the eight little stick crosses in the ground behind the holes. And then we went and got Tom, and then me and Suzanne and Tom went and got Joe-down-the-road.

●⟩ ●⟩ ●⟩

The crisp packet that Joe had put under a stone to show where the Old Rabbit was buried wasn't there anymore. But Joe said he knew exactly where it was anyway, and he pointed to the spot.

I started to dig. I didn't dig with the trowel like I did for the eight hamster holes because Joe said I might dig through the Old Rabbit.

131

So I dug with my hands, and after a while I could feel something hard. I flicked all the mud off the hard thing, and I could feel that the hard thing had fur on. The Old Rabbit looked very old in the ground. And it smelled.

Joe said he hoped there weren't any worms, and there weren't, but there were some maggots because some of them fell out of the Old Rabbit's mouth when I got it out of the ground. But Joe didn't see, and I brushed the mud away from the Old Rabbit's face, and out of its eyes before I showed it to him. And I showed him the side with the closed eye because on the other side the eye was still open, and it had gone a bit funny, and I didn't think Joe would like it.

Joe stroked the Old Rabbit on its nose, and he wiped its body with Suzanne's hankie, and made

its fur all smooth, and then he
held the Old Rabbit to his cheek,
and after that he put the Old
Rabbit in the box, on the straw, and
Suzanne put a dandelion in, and I
put the lid on, and I put the box in the ground,
and I covered it over, and Suzanne put a cross in
the ground behind it.

And then Joe said he had to go because even
though he liked the Old Rabbit best, the New Cat
might be hunting the New Rabbit for all he knew,
and he had to go back to sit on the hutch with his
Super Soaker, just in case.

Suzanne put the eight Baby Hamsters in the
ground and I covered them over. Suzanne said
we should all say something about the Baby
Hamsters. I didn't want to say anything about

them because I couldn't really think of anything except that they looked a bit like prawns, and I didn't want to say that. But Suzanne said it wasn't really a proper funeral if no one said anything.

So Suzanne said, 'They didn't look like hamsters but they were. They just hadn't got their fur yet.'

Which was true.

And I said, 'They were born in the night and in the morning they were dead.'

Which was also true.

And Tom said, 'They are under the mud.'

Which was true as well. And which was better than at Nanna's funeral because there the Vicar kept saying how Nanna never had a bad word to say about anyone. And that wasn't true because Nanna did have a bad word to say about some people sometimes. Like Suzanne's Dad, and Miss Matheson, and Joe-down-the-road's Mum's Boyfriend. But she never said a bad word about me, or Tom, or Vera off 'Coronation Street'.

CHAPTER 17
A Real Investigation

In the morning, when Suzanne knocked on the wall three times, me and Tom were ready. We met at the shed at eight o'clock and Suzanne said we should call it 'Oh, Eight Hundred Hours', so we did. Suzanne's Mum watches all the police dramas on telly, and Suzanne does too, even the late ones that I'm not allowed to watch, and that's how Suzanne knows all about exactly what you should call things in a Real Investigation.

Suzanne said the first thing we should do was have a meeting. The password was Investigation. Tom didn't like the password being Investigation at first because it's quite a hard word, because he's only five, and he kept calling it 'In-ges-tiv-ation'.

I said it didn't matter if Tom got the password a little bit wrong, as long as it was nearly right.

And Suzanne said it didn't really even matter if he couldn't remember it at all, because he could just say, 'Hello, it's me, Tom' like he always does, because he always ends up forgetting what the password is anyway.

After we had the meeting and decided on the password, I said I thought we should go and see Mrs Rotherham up the road because she would know what to do because she used to be in the police.

Tom didn't want to go because he is scared of Mrs Rotherham. He thought we should go in the house and see Mum and have a biscuit instead. But Suzanne said that having a biscuit definitely wasn't the next thing to do.

I'm not scared of Mrs Rotherham. I wasn't that scared of her in the first place but I'm really not scared of her now because at Nanna's funeral, Mrs Rotherham gave me her hankie and, after I'd blown my nose on it, she said I could keep it. It's a really old hankie, probably about a hundred years old or something, and it's got lace on. Mrs Rotherham made it herself.

Anyway, Mum hadn't told Mrs Rotherham any of the bad things about me and Tom that she always said she had half a mind to. Or, if she had, Mrs Rotherham didn't seem to care. Mrs Rotherham winked at me when the Vicar was saying how Nanna never said a bad word about anyone. And afterwards she showed me how to wink. I can only do it with one eye. I'm practising with the other one. Mrs Rotherham said I could come to her house whenever I liked.

Tom said he would come up the road with me and Suzanne as long as he could wait outside. So that is what we did.

Mrs Rotherham's house smells of old things, and mothballs, the same as Nanna's used to. Most old ladies' houses smell a bit the same when they are really old. It's a funny smell, a bit like the old cupboard upstairs at Sunday School. Our house will probably smell like that soon because Mum keeps finding grey hairs on her head and that means she must be nearly old too.

Anyway, I told Mrs Rotherham all about what happened to the hamsters. Mrs Rotherham said, 'Well, well, well.' And then she said 'Oh dear, oh dear, oh dear.' Which Suzanne said afterwards is what police people used to say in the olden days. And then she said, 'A *massacre!*'

I told Mrs Rotherham all about what The Vet had said about how she thought that Number Two had bitten Number One's leg off, and how she thought Number One had killed all the babies, and how she thought Number Two had escaped.

Mrs Rotherham said, 'The Vet is probably right.'

And I said 'Oh,' because for one thing that wasn't really what I wanted Mrs Rotherham to say, and for another thing it didn't really help us with our investigation.

Suzanne told Mrs Rotherham how we were doing an investigation, and how we thought Mrs Rotherham might be able to help because, she said, 'Maybe The Vet *wasn't* right, and maybe someone else killed the hamsters, and maybe seeing as how you used to be in the Police, you could help us catch whoever it was by telling us what to do in a Real Investigation.'

Mrs Rotherham said, 'I see. The Vet probably is right. But, in a Real Investigation, probably is not good enough. *Probably* doesn't come into it.'

And then she winked.

'The first thing to do in a Real Investigation – particularly a murder investigation – and particularly a mass-murder investigation, such as this one, is to get yourself a nice cup of tea, and a biscuit.'

And she went into the kitchen. After a while she came back with the tea, and with some biscuits, and she poured the tea out, and she put the milk in, and the sugars, because she said sweet tea was best for this sort of thing. And she drank her tea, and we drank our tea.

And then she said, 'Is your brother going to come in?'

I said he wasn't.

Mrs Rotherham said, 'Only it's raining.'

And I said, 'Tom doesn't mind if it's raining.'

Which he didn't.

'Because,' I said, 'once me and Tom went out and stood in the rain for ages on purpose to see how wet we could get and we got really, really wet and that was about the best thing Tom said he had ever done…'

Suzanne said we didn't have time to talk about Tom and the rain, and we had to get on with the investigation.

Mrs Rotherham said, 'Quite right.' And she looked very serious. And then she said, 'You will need these.' And she gave us a small notepad and a pencil. And then she said, 'And you might need this.' And she gave us a magnifying glass. And then she said, 'And this.' And she gave us a Dictaphone, which is a thing for recording what people say, and it's got a little tape inside. And then she said, 'And you will definitely need this', and she

gave us a real police badge. And then Mrs Rotherham wrote on a piece of paper for quite a long time. And she put the piece of paper in an envelope. And she wrote 'Investigation Instructions' on the envelope and she gave the envelope to Suzanne. And she gave me three biscuits to give to Tom.

And then she said, 'I'll expect you back before tea-time.'

Tom was still waiting outside, and he was quite wet, especially his feet because he was waiting in a puddle. But he didn't mind, and he was very pleased about the biscuits, especially when we told him that Mrs Rotherham said that tea and biscuits were the first things that you should do in a Real Investigation. Because Tom said he thought that they might be.

And then me and Suzanne and Tom went back to the shed.

⋆ CHAPTER 18 ⋆
Who Done It?

Suzanne opened the envelope and she read out what it said on the piece of paper. And then I read out what it said on the piece of paper again because Suzanne isn't all that good at reading sometimes, and Mrs Rotherham's handwriting was quite curly like Nanna's used to be, like old people always write, and it was quite shaky too, and Suzanne kept getting the words wrong.

The first thing it said on Mrs Rotherham's piece of paper was…

MAKE A LIST OF SUSPECTS
To do this you will need...

a) Your notepad and pencil

b) Your brain

You must ask yourself the following questions:

1. Who do you think might have murdered the hamsters?

2. Have they done or said anything that makes you suspect them?

3. Do they have any prior record of violence or murder? (This means have they done something like it before)

(Tip: A hunch is as good a reason as any to make someone a suspect.)

We thought of some suspects and I wrote them down. We had eight suspects altogether. We did have nine but then Suzanne said she thought we should take one of them off, which was the Fox, because she said, 'No one has seen a fox in the street, and a fox would be too big to get in through the cat flap, and it wouldn't be able to get in the house any other way.'

I said, 'I think a fox might be able to get through the cat flap, if it was a very skinny one.'

But Tom said, 'I am smaller than a fox, and *I* can't get through the cat flap because I have tried lots of times and I always get stuck.'

So this is what it said on our suspects list…

ANNA'S AND SUZANNE'S AND TOM'S LIST OF SUSPECTS FOR THE HAMSTER MASSACRE INVESTIGATION

1. Mr Tucker

Because...

a) He doesn't like Russians

b) He called the hamsters "Gremlins"

2. Joe-down-the-road's Mum's Boyfriend

Because...

a) We have got a hunch

b) ?

3. Hamster Number Two

Because...

a) He used to bite a lot and he could have bitten Number One's leg off and killed the babies and escaped

4. The New Cat

Because...

a) She is always crouching near my bedroom door in a hunting kind of way

b) She has already killed four Sparrows, three Field Mice, five Moths, eight Spiders, one Bumble Bee and scared the Old Rabbit to death

5. Mum

Because...

a) She didn't want the hamsters in the first place

b) She has already killed two hamsters called Geoff and Bernard

6. Suzanne's Dad

Because...

a) He 'HATES PETS'

7. Hamster Number One

Because...

a) She was in the cage at the time

b) The Vet said so

c) Mum said so

d) Dad said so

e) The internet said so

f) The chapter called 'Severely Stressed Hamsters' in the *Hamsters — A Manual* book said so.

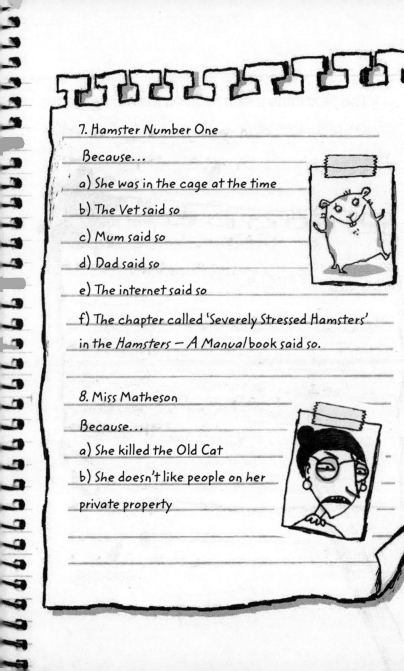

8. Miss Matheson

Because...

a) She killed the Old Cat

b) She doesn't like people on her private property

The next thing it said to do on Mrs Rotherham's piece of paper after making a list of suspects was…

INTERVIEW YOUR SUSPECTS

To do this you will need...

1) Your police badge

2) Your notepad and pencil

3) Your Dictaphone to record the interviews

4) Your magnifying glass to look for clues

You should...

1. Ask the suspects where they were when the massacre was committed.

2. Ask them to prove that they were where they say they were (Do they have an alibi? Was someone with them at the time?)

3. If they have a solid alibi you must eliminate them from your investigation (cross them off the suspect list).

This is what it says an alibi is in my dictionary...

alibi [al-uh-by] ✦ *noun*
proof that someone who is thought to have committed a crime could not have done it, especially the fact or claim that they were in another place at the time it happened.

153

We didn't check what it said in the dictionary in Suzanne's house because for one thing the dictionary in Suzanne's house always ends up getting us into trouble, and for another thing my dictionary sounded like it had the right kind of alibi in it. We decided I would be the one to tell people what had happened with the hamsters, and to press record on the Dictaphone when people started talking, because I was the only one with pockets big enough to fit the Dictaphone in, and if people knew they were being recorded they might not like it. And Suzanne would be the one to hold the real police badge and ask the questions and write in the notepad. And Tom would be the one to hold the magnifying glass and look for clues.

The first suspect on our list was Mr Tucker.

I didn't really want to go to Mr Tucker's house first because I thought we might get stuck talking about litter and everything, but Tom said he wanted to see Mr Tucker anyway and Suzanne said that she would hold up the police badge and tell Mr Tucker that we didn't have time to talk about litter.

So we went and knocked on Mr Tucker's door.

●? ●? ●?

I told Mr Tucker how the eight Baby Hamsters were dead and how Number Two was missing and how Number One only had three legs left.

Mr Tucker said, 'Good God! A wilding! You had better come in. If you ask me—'

But Suzanne got the police badge out.

And she said, 'Mr Tucker. Where were your whereabouts between the hours of two a.m. and seven a.m. on Thursday morning?'

Mr Tucker said, 'So, that's how it is, eh?'

And he sat down and said, 'In bed. Civvy kip. Where else should an old lag be?'

Tom put the magnifying glass up close to Mr Tucker's face and looked him up and down. Mr Tucker's eye bulged through the glass.

Mr Tucker said, 'A snoop! Tom! I didn't have you down for that, Old Chum.'

Suzanne said, 'Was anyone else in bed with you?'

And Mr Tucker said, 'Mrs Tucker, of course. Upstart!'

And then he shouted up the stairs, **'DICKEY. COME DOWN, WILL YOU!'**

And Mrs Tucker came down.

Mr Tucker said, 'Now, Dickey, don't fold up. Give 'em a good show, and for God's sake keep doggo about the bodies out the back.' And then he pulled faces at Tom through the magnifying glass.

Suzanne said, 'Name?' to Mrs Tucker.

And Mrs Tucker said, 'Dickey Tucker.'

And then we had to stop for a bit because Suzanne had to go the toilet.

When Suzanne came back from the toilet, Mrs Tucker said that Mr Tucker was definitely in bed asleep between two a.m. and seven a.m. on Thursday, because she was there too, and she is a very light sleeper, and she said, 'Mr Tucker

157

snores a lot, and thrashes about, and shouts out, and I was wide awake reading. I haven't slept more than four hours a night since 1945.'

I was not sure Mrs Tucker was telling the truth but she took her glasses off and pointed to the bags under her eyes, and Tom looked at them with the magnifying glass, and they were very big. And then Mr Tucker pretended to fall asleep in the chair and he did lots of snoring and he shouted, 'We're hit. We're hit. One engine down. Come in, Charlie!'

And Tom thought that was the best thing ever and he laughed a lot.

And then Mr Tucker picked Tom up, and flew him round the room.

And then he sat down because Mrs Tucker said, 'Stop it, Raymond! You'll give yourself a heart attack.'

And then she went to get some lemonade.

We drank the lemonade and said, 'thank you' to Mrs Tucker. And then we crossed Mr Tucker off the Suspect List.

The next person on our list was Joe-down-the-road's Mum's Boyfriend. Because we had a hunch about him. And Mrs Rotherham had said that a hunch was as good a reason as any.

Joe was sitting on the New Rabbit's hutch in the backyard with the Super Soaker. We asked Joe if his Mum's Boyfriend was there. But Joe didn't answer. Joe never answers if he doesn't want to.

159

Joe's Mum was standing looking out of the back window.

I told Joe's Mum about what had happened with the hamsters and how we were asking people if they had seen anything unusual and Suzanne said, 'Can you tell us where your boyfriend's whereabouts were between two a.m. and seven a.m. on Thursday?'

And Joe's Mum said, 'I can tell you *exactly* where his whereabouts were between two a.m. and seven a.m. on Thursday. His whereabouts were in Kuala bloomin' Lumpur. In the Mandarin Oriental Hotel. And the babysitter's whereabouts were there as well!'

And she showed us Kuala Lumpur on Joe's globe. It's a long way away.

KUALA
LUMPUR

And then she showed us her Boyfriend's bank statement. And Tom looked at it through the magnifying glass. It said,

£ BANK STATEMENT

Date	payment type and details	paid out
30 Aug	DELUXE SUITE, MANDARIN ORIENTAL, KUALA LUMPUR	£268.50

We said thank you to Joe's Mum, and she gave Tom a biscuit, because he asked for one. And we crossed her Boyfriend off the list.

●; ●; ●;

The next suspect on the list was Hamster Number Two. We couldn't interview Number Two because he was still missing. And even though we had put trails of food out every night, he hadn't come back yet.

So Suzanne wrote 'missing' next to Number Two's name on the Suspect List. And we went to find the New Cat.

●: ●: ●:

It was a bit difficult to interview the New Cat because of her being a cat, and because she couldn't answer the questions, but Tom said he just wanted to look the New Cat in the eye with the magnifying glass to see if he could tell anything by that.

The New Cat looked even angrier than ever through the magnifying glass. She hissed at Tom and made her fur go big. And then Tom tried to pick the New Cat up. And the New Cat bit Tom really hard. And then Tom bit the New Cat back, even harder. And the New Cat looked very surprised because no one had ever bitten her back before. And Tom looked quite surprised too because he had never bitten a cat before either. And also because he had quite a lot of the New Cat's fur in his mouth.

Tom said he wanted to go and see Mum to get the fur out of his mouth. And Mum was the next person on our list anyway. So that is what we did.

Mum didn't really like being questioned. She made Tom put the magnifying glass down, and she made Suzanne put the notepad down. But she didn't make me turn the Dictaphone off because she didn't know it was on record in my pocket.

Mum said, 'We've been through all this already. You know fine well that I was in bed. And that I didn't hear anything. This is getting beyond a joke.'

I said 'It never was a joke,' because it wasn't.

I said, 'It's an investigation.'

But Mum said, 'It's not healthy. All this digging about death. And you shouldn't be dragging poor Suzanne into it.'

Suzanne said how she wasn't being dragged into it because she was in charge, actually.

But Mum said, 'The *investigation* is *over*. If you don't drop it, right now, and accept that Number One killed the babies, and Number Two bit her leg off and escaped, then I am sending Suzanne home. And I'm going to phone Mrs Rotherham because I'm cross that she is encouraging all of this.'

So we promised that we would drop it, and that we wouldn't investigate anyone else, and we crossed Mum off the list.

And we just went to investigate Suzanne's Dad and Number One and Miss Matheson very quickly because they were the only suspects left.

When we got to Suzanne's house, Suzanne's Dad was in the bathroom. Suzanne banged on the door.

Suzanne's Dad shouted, **'I'M ON THE TOILET, FOR CRYING OUT LOUD!'**

Suzanne said that her Dad sometimes sits on the toilet for hours. We didn't have time to wait for him to get off the toilet, especially because

Suzanne said she didn't think her Dad was in a very good mood anyway, not enough to be asked about his whereabouts, so we asked Suzanne's Mum instead.

I told Suzanne's Mum all about what had happened with the hamsters and everything.

Suzanne's Mum said My Mum had already told her.

Suzanne said, 'Yes, but can you tell us about where Dad's whereabouts were between two a.m. and seven a.m. on Thursday morning?'

Suzanne's Mum said, 'Yes. He was here. Up and down with his piles all night.'

I said, 'What are piles?'

Suzanne's Mum said, 'I haven't got time to stand around talking about piles all day. You get them in your bottom. They aren't very nice.'

This is what it says about piles in the dictionary in Suzanne's house…

> **piles** ✦ *noun*
> swollen and painful varicose veins in the canal of the anus also known as haemorrhoids

We crossed Suzanne's Dad off the list and we went to see Hamster Number One.

Number One was in the nest. I peeled back the top of the nest and picked Number One up and stroked her on the head. I could feel the stitches where her leg used to be. Number One looked very thin, and her fur was all matted, and she didn't even open her eyes.

I said, 'I think Number One is too sick to be interviewed.'

Tom looked at Number One through the magnifying glass. And he said that he thought so too.

I gave Number One a kiss on the head, and put her back in the nest, and Suzanne wrote 'Sick' next to her name on the Suspect List, and said we should come back when Number One was better.

And then we went to see Miss Matheson.

Miss Matheson didn't take the chain off when she answered the door. I told her what had happened to the hamsters through the crack.

Suzanne showed Miss Matheson the real police badge and said, 'We need to know where your whereabouts were between two a.m. and seven a.m. on Thursday, Miss Matheson.'

Miss Matheson took the chain off the door and said, **'GET OFF MY PROPERTY BEFORE I CALL THE POLICE! I WARNED YOU ABOUT ALL THIS LAST TIME WITH THAT AWFUL OLD CAT. THIS IS TRESPASS. I'VE KEPT A RECORD!'**

So we ran up the road to Mrs Rotherham's because we were already late and because it was seventeen hundred and a half hours and that is after tea-time.

And Tom said he would come into Mrs Rotherham's house with us because he wasn't scared of her anymore and because he liked her biscuits.

🐾 CHAPTER 19 🐾
The Hysterics

Mrs Rotherham loved it when we played her all the interviews on the Dictaphone. She said it was the best thing she had ever heard in her life. Mrs Rotherham got The Hysterics.

Me and Tom and Suzanne got The Hysterics a bit too, but not as much as Mrs Rotherham.

Mrs Rotherham got The Hysterics all the way through. She got them so badly she had to lie on the floor. She said it was a shame that Nanna wasn't there because Nanna would have got The Hysterics as well. And she would. Because it was almost as funny as when Graham Roberts was Jesus, just in his pants.

Tom said, 'Nanna said ice cream is good when you need to calm down.'

And Mrs Rotherham went and got some out of the freezer.

After we ate the ice cream, and Mrs Rotherham calmed down, Suzanne showed Mrs Rotherham the Suspect List.

Mrs Rotherham said, 'So, Mr Tucker, Joe-down-the-road's Mum's Boyfriend, Your Mum, and Suzanne's Dad all have solid alibis and are eliminated from the investigation, which means that it had to be either Hamster Number One, or Hamster Number Two, or The New Cat, or Miss Matheson who committed the massacre.'

Mrs Rotherham's phone rang.

Mrs Rotherham answered the phone and said, 'Hello.' And then she said, 'It's your Mum.' And then she winked.

And then she spoke into the phone and said, 'Ah. I see. Leave it with me. Goodbye.'

Mrs Rotherham put the phone down. She looked very serious.

And she said, 'I must inform you that

the Investigation into the Hamster Massacre, although unsolved, is now, and until further notice, officially closed.'

I said, 'Why?'

Mrs Rotherham said, 'The usual reasons: lack of funding, and manpower, and evidence, and missing and uncooperative suspects and witnesses. And because it's unlikely that new evidence will come to light at this late stage. Those are the main reasons.

'And also because Miss Matheson has called Your Mum to complain, and also because your tea is ready.'

Tom said, 'Let's go home', because he didn't want to do an investigation anymore because he was hungry, and he needed a wee, and because, he said, 'It's probably Miss Matheson that did the murder anyway. It was her the last time.'

I said, 'Suzanne found cat blood on her tyres.'

And Mrs Rotherham said, 'Well done.'

Suzanne said, 'It was red.'

Tom said, 'Have you got any biscuits?'

Mrs Rotherham said she did. And she gave Tom a biscuit, and Tom gave her back the magnifying glass, and I gave her the Dictaphone, and Suzanne gave her the police badge but Mrs Rotherham said we could keep the notebook. And she said we should come back whenever we wanted, and especially if there was ever another investigation.

And Suzanne said, 'There probably will be.'

Because there quite often is.

And we went back to the shed and we put the investigation notebook next to the worm box and the wasp trap and the pictures that we traced from Joe-down-the-road's Mum's book.

❝ CHAPTER 20 ❞
What I Did In My Summer Holidays

So that's pretty much everything that has happened with the hamsters and everything. Except that Number One died in the night. It was three days after Mrs Rotherham closed the Real Investigation.

We didn't really do a funeral for Number One because for one thing Tom said he was sick of doing funerals, and for another thing I couldn't think of anything to say. Suzanne says if you don't say something it isn't really a funeral at all, which is true.

I buried Number One on my own. I dug a hole next to the eight Baby Hamsters and I put her in

there. I put her in a box but I didn't
decorate it. And I
didn't put a cross
in the ground
either.

Mum said I could get another hamster if I
wanted to. Just one. On its own. But I don't really
want to. Tom says he doesn't want to either
because he said the New Cat wouldn't like it.
I don't really care about the New Cat but ever
since Tom bit the New Cat back, Tom does.

That's when the New Cat started following Tom
around. The New Cat follows Tom everywhere
now, even when he's busy holding the bin bag
for Mr Tucker, or walking in a straight line with
his eyes closed, or collecting gravel, the New
Cat goes too. I don't think I would like it if the

New Cat followed *me* around. But Tom does. Sometimes the New Cat sleeps on Tom's bed. And sometimes it puts dead things on his pillow.

I won't sleep in Tom's bed anymore because for one thing I don't like it that the New Cat might put a dead thing in it, and for another thing I'm too old to sleep in Tom's bed really, because I'm nine, and for an even other thing it's school again tomorrow. And you have to sleep in your own bed when it's school again.

I really am supposed to be doing my What-I-Did-In-My-Summer-Holidays Story for school now. I still can't remember any nice things to put in it. But, like Mum says, I can just make some nice things up because it's only a holiday story. So it doesn't really matter if it's not exactly true. Not like when you're writing up a Real Investigation. You can't make anything up at all when you're writing one of those. With a Real Investigation you have to write everything exactly right. And you have to write it straight away. That's what Suzanne says. And that's what I did.

The End

If you enjoyed THE GREAT HAMSTER MASSACRE,
look out for the next book about Anna,
Suzanne, Tom and Joe-down-the-road...
Here's an extract from
THE GREAT RABBIT RESCUE,
coming soon!

Me and Suzanne peered into the hutch to have a look at the New Rabbit. There was a lot of hay in the way, all piled up against the wire mesh at the front. Suzanne reached her hand in through the hay and felt around.

"Oh," she said, "I can feel it. It's all soft and fluffy and warm."

And then she screamed, "AGH!" and she

pulled her hand back. Her finger was bleeding. She put it in her mouth.

"It bit me!" she said.

I said, "Maybe it was asleep, and it got frightened when you put your hand in." Because when me and Tom had hamsters, we had this book, called *Hamsters - A Manual*, which said that hamsters only bite when they're frightened. Which you would be if a giant hand was coming at you from above. And it's probably the same with rabbits.

So I said, "Things only bite when they're frightened."

And Suzanne said, "No, they don't. Some things bite because they like it."

And I said, "Like what?"

And Suzanne said, "Like the New Cat!"

I said, "The New Cat is different. You don't get rabbits like that. Rabbits just hop around, and eat lettuce, and fall asleep, and wear yellow ribbons on Easter cards and things."

Suzanne took her finger out of her mouth. It was still bleeding.

She said, "You put *your* hand in its hutch, then."

And I said, "I will."

I undid the latch and opened the hutch door a crack and put my hand in very slowly and lay it flat on the bottom of the hutch, like the hamster manual said you should. So that the rabbit would be curious and come and smell my hand, instead of being frightened and biting, like it did with Suzanne. We heard something rustle, but

we couldn't see the rabbit through the hay. And then I felt the rabbit's fur against my hand, and its whiskers. I kept my hand very still. And I said, "It's sniffing my hand. It tickles."

And then I said, "*Nice* New Rabbit."

And then I said, "AGH!"

And I jumped, and pulled my hand out. And put my finger in my mouth. And then I said, "It bit me!"

And Suzanne said, "*See.*"

And she put the latch back on.

The New Rabbit rustled in the hay. And it pushed its way through it to the front of the hutch. It was white. And it had pink eyes. And it was *Absolutely Enormous*. The New Rabbit stared out at us through the wire mesh.

Suzanne said, "Look at its *eyes!*"

And I said, "Look at its *ears!*"

And Suzanne said, "Look at its *teeth!*"

And I said, "Look at its *claws!*"

And Suzanne said, "When did it get so *big?*"

Because the last time me and Suzanne had seen the New Rabbit, it was tiny. And its eyes were closed. And it fitted in Joe's hands.

But me and Suzanne hadn't seen the New Rabbit for ages. Because even when we used to help Joe-down-the-road guard the New Rabbit, we hardly ever saw it, because it was always in its hutch, hiding behind the hay.

The New Rabbit gnawed on the wire on the front of the hutch. It had long yellow teeth.

Suzanne said, "It's not like Joe's *Old* Rabbit, is it?"

And it wasn't, because if you put your hand in

the Old Rabbit's hutch, the Old Rabbit would rub its head against you, and hop onto your hand to be taken out. And then, if you let it, it would go up your jumper and nuzzle your neck, which was what it liked best. You couldn't fit the New Rabbit up your jumper. Not even if you wanted to. And you wouldn't want to anyway because the New Rabbit looked very angry.

We looked at the New Rabbit. And the New Rabbit looked back at us. Suzanne said, "It's too big for the hutch."

And it was, because it was almost as big as the hutch itself.

I said, "Maybe that's why it's angry."

Because the Old Rabbit had lots of room to hop around in the hutch. But if the New Rabbit stretched out, its feet would touch both ends.

I said, "We could let it out for a bit."

And Suzanne said, "How will we get it back in?"

And I said, "We won't let it *out* out. We'll just let it out in the run. Only for a minute. And then we'll shoo it back in."

And Suzanne said, "Good idea."

Which Suzanne hardly ever says, so that means it was.

We picked up the run from the corner of the garden. And we put it on the front of the hutch. And it fitted just right. Because that's how Joe's Dad had made it, ages ago, for the Old Rabbit, when he still lived with Joe and Joe's Mum.

There was a small hole in the wire mesh, in one corner of the run. We looked at the hole, and we looked at the rabbit. The hole was about the size of a jam jar. And the rabbit was about the size of a dog. In fact it was bigger than a dog. It was bigger than Miss Matheson's dog anyway, much bigger, because that's only the same size as a guinea pig. Anyway, the rabbit was definitely bigger than the hole. So we opened the door of the hutch. And the rabbit hopped out into the run. And it stood very still in the middle of the run, and it sniffed the air, and it put its ears right up. And then it hopped over to the corner with the hole. And it looked at the hole. And then, in a second, it squeezed through.

Suzanne said, "It's out!"

And I said, "The gate!"

And I ran to the gate and got there just before the rabbit did. And I slammed it shut. The rabbit looked angrier than ever. And it thumped its back leg on the ground. I tried to grab the rabbit. And

Suzanne tried to grab the rabbit. But whenever we got near it, the New Rabbit ran at us and bit and scrabbled and scratched.

I said, "We need gardening gloves." Like Mum uses to put the New Cat in its carry case when it has to go to the vet.

And I ran up the road to the shed, and got the gardening gloves, and put them on, and ran back down.

When I got back, Suzanne was running round Joe's garden in circles, and the New Rabbit was running after her. I told Suzanne to turn around and run at the rabbit, to shoo it towards me, so I could pick it up with the gardening gloves. And she did.

I grabbed hold of the rabbit. And it scrabbled and scratched and clawed and kicked. But I held onto it, tight. And then it bit me, hard, right through

the gloves. And I dropped it.

I said, "It bit me! Right through the gardening gloves."

I could see a patch of blood. So I ran back up the road, and I got some plasters, and my big brother Andy's cricket pads, and the helmet for his bike, and I put them on. And I got his shin pads, and his gum shield, and some old oven gloves and a balaclava for Suzanne. And I also got two fishing nets.

When I got back, Suzanne was in the corner of Joe's garden, pressed against the fence, and the New Rabbit was in front of her, and it was making a growling sound, and there were scratches all over her legs.

I said, "I didn't know rabbits growled."

And Suzanne said, "HELP!"

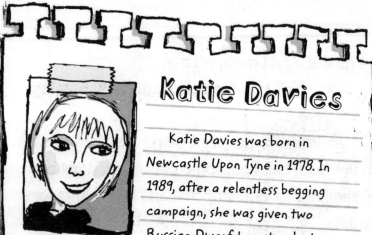

Katie Davies

Katie Davies was born in Newcastle Upon Tyne in 1978. In 1989, after a relentless begging campaign, she was given two Russian Dwarf hamsters by her Mum for Christmas. She is yet to recover from what happened to those hamsters. THE GREAT HAMSTER MASSACRE is Katie's first novel. She is currently working on its sequel, THE GREAT RABBIT RESCUE. Katie now lives in North London with her husband, the comedian, Alan Davies. She does not have any hamsters.

Hannah Shaw

Hannah Shaw was born into a large family of sprout-munching vegetarians. She spent her formative years trying to be good at everything; from roller-skating to gymnastics, but she soon realised there wasn't much chance of her becoming a gold medal winning gymnast, so she resigned herself to writing stories and drawing pictures instead!

Hannah currently lives in a little cottage in the Cotswolds, with her husband Ben the blacksmith and her rescue dog Ren. She finds her over-active imagination fuels new ideas but unfortunately keeps her awake at night!